W9-ALZ-884

FIVE Little MONKEYS
5-Minute Stories

Eileen Christelow

Houghton Mifflin Harcourt
Boston   New York

Compilation copyright © 2018 by Eileen Christelow
All rights reserved.

FIVE LITTLE MONKEYS is a registered trademark of Houghton Mifflin Harcourt Publishing Company, and the monkey logo is a trademark of Houghton Mifflin Harcourt Publishing Company.

Five Little Monkeys Jumping on the Bed © 1989 by Eileen Christelow
Five Little Monkeys Sitting in a Tree © 1991 by Eileen Christelow
Five Little Monkeys with Nothing to Do © 1991 by Eileen Christelow
Five Little Monkeys Bake a Birthday Cake © 1992 by Eileen Christelow
Five Little Monkeys Wash the Car © 2000 by Eileen Christelow
Five Little Monkeys Play Hide-and-Seek © 2004 by Eileen Christelow
Five Little Monkeys Jump in the Bath © 2012 by Eileen Christelow
Five Little Monkeys Reading in Bed © 2011 by Eileen Christelow

Houghton Mifflin Harcourt
125 High Street
Boston, MA 02110

hmhco.com
ISBN: 978-1-328-45359-4

Manufactured in China
LEO 10 9 8 7 6 5 4 3 2 1
4500685320

Contents

Five Little Monkeys
Jumping on the Bed

It was bedtime.
So five little monkeys took a bath.

Five little monkeys put on their pajamas.

Five little monkeys brushed their teeth.

Five little monkeys said good night to their mama.

Then . . . five little monkeys
jumped on the bed!

One fell off and bumped his head.

The mama called the doctor. The doctor said,

"No more monkeys jumping on the bed!"

So four little monkeys . . .

. . .jumped on the bed.

One fell off and bumped his head.

The mama called the doctor.

The doctor said,

"No more monkeys jumping on the bed!"

So three little monkeys jumped on the bed.

One fell off and bumped her head.

The mama called the doctor.

The doctor said,

"No more monkeys jumping on the bed!"

So two little monkeys jumped on the bed.

One fell off and bumped his head.

The mama called the doctor.   The doctor said,

"No more monkeys jumping on the bed!"

So one little monkey jumped on the bed.

She fell off and bumped her head.

The mama called the doctor.

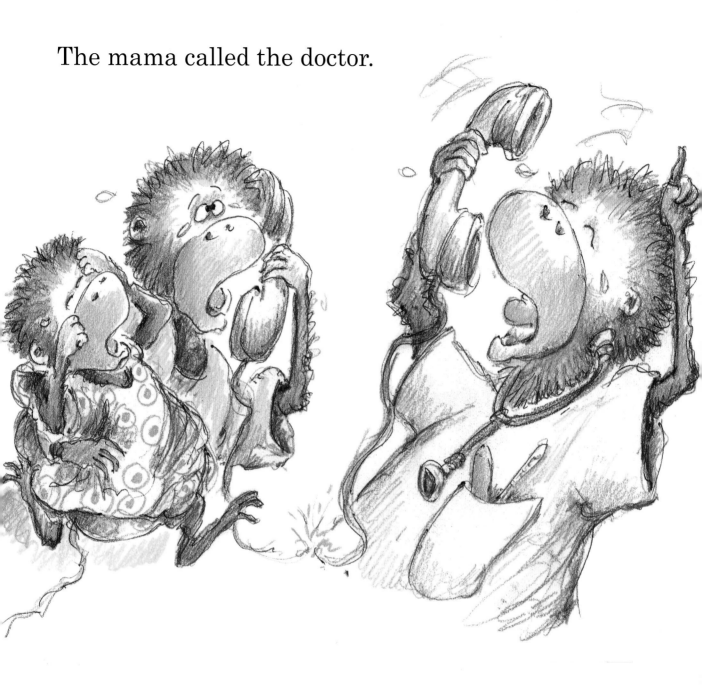

The doctor said,

"NO MORE MONKEYS JUMPING ON THE BED!"

So five little monkeys fell fast asleep.

"Thank goodness!" said the mama.

"Now I can go to bed!"

Five Little Monkeys Sitting in a Tree

Five little monkeys and their mama
walk down to the river for a picnic supper.

Mama spreads out a blanket
and settles down for a snooze . . .

. . . while five little monkeys
climb a tree to watch Mr. Crocodile.

Five little monkeys, sitting in a tree,
tease Mr. Crocodile, "Can't catch me!"

Along comes Mr. Crocodile . . .

Oh no! Where is she?

Four little monkeys, sitting in a tree,
tease Mr. Crocodile, "Can't catch me."
Along comes Mr. Crocodile . . .

Oh no!
Where is he?

Three little monkeys, sitting in a tree,
tease Mr. Crocodile, "Can't catch me!"
Along comes Mr. Crocodile . . .

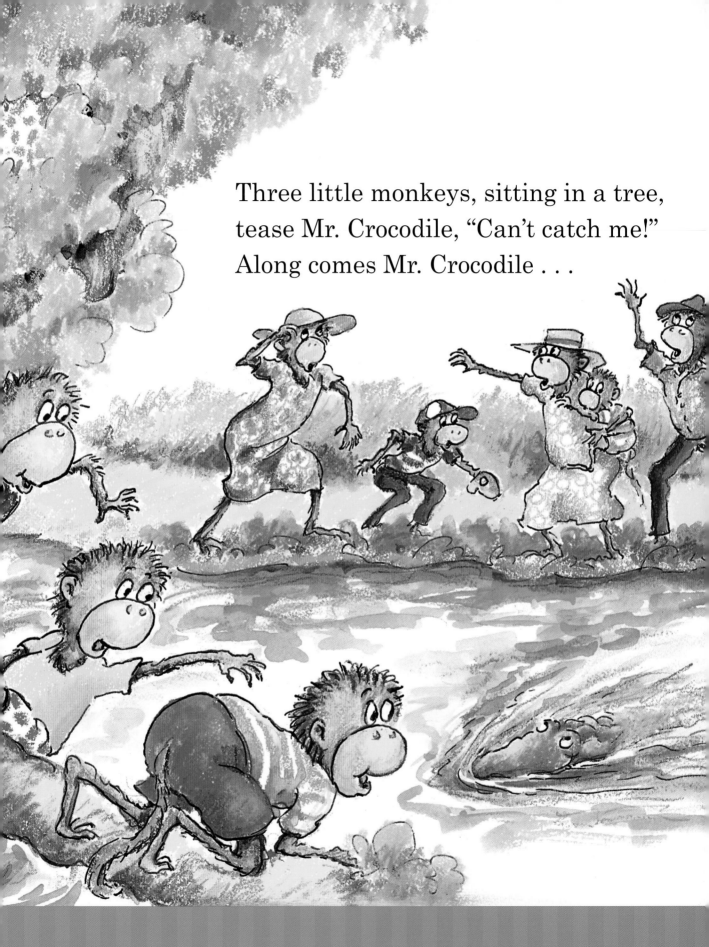

Oh no! Where is he?

Two little monkeys, sitting in a tree,
tease Mr. Crocodile, "Can't catch me!"
Along comes Mr. Crocodile . . .

Oh no! Where is she?

Now there's only one little
monkey, sitting in the tree,
teasing Mr. Crocodile,
"Can't catch me!"
Along comes Mr. Crocodile …

Oh no! There are no little monkeys sitting in the tree. But, wait! Look!

1 2 3 4 5

Five little monkeys, sitting in the tree!

Their mama
hugs them.

Their mama scolds them.
"Never tease a crocodile.
It's not nice—and it's dangerous."

Then five little monkeys and their mama
eat a delicious picnic supper.

And they do not tease Mr. Crocodile again!

Five Little Monkeys
with Nothing to Do

It is summer. There is no school.
Five little monkeys tell their mama,
"We're bored. There is nothing to do!"

"Oh yes there is," says Mama.
"Grandma Bessie is coming for lunch,
and the house must be neat and clean.

"So . . . you can pick up your room."

Five little monkeys pick up
and pick up and pick up . . .

. . . until everything is put away.

"Good job!" says Mama.
"But we're bored again," say five little monkeys.
"There is nothing to do!"

"Oh yes there is," says Mama.
"You can scrub the bathroom. The house
must be neat and clean for Grandma Bessie."

So five little monkeys scrub and scrub . . .

... and scrub until the bathroom shines.

"Good job!" says Mama.

"But we're bored again," say five little monkeys.

"There is nothing to do!"

"Oh yes there is," says Mama.
"You can beat the dirt out of these rugs. The
house must be nice and clean for Grandma Bessie."

Five little monkeys beat and beat and beat the rugs . . .

. . . until there is not a speck of dirt left.

"Good job!" says Mama.

"But we're bored again," say five little monkeys.

"There is nothing to do!"

"Oh yes there is," says Mama.
"You can pick some berries down by the swamp.
Grandma Bessie loves berries for dessert."

Five little monkeys run down
to the muddy, muddy swamp.

They pick and pick and pick berries
until Mama calls, "It's time to come home!"

Five little monkeys run inside
while Mama picks flowers.

"Put the berries in the kitchen," calls Mama.
"Wash your faces and put on clean clothes."

Five little monkeys wash their faces . . .

. . . and they put on clean clothes.

"Grandma is here!" calls Mama.

Five little monkeys race outside.

They hug and kiss Grandma Bessie.
"We've been busy all day!" they say. "We cleaned
the house and picked berries just for you!"

"I love berries," says Grandma Bessie.
"And I love a clean house, too!"
They all go inside.

"Oh my!" says Grandma Bessie.
"Oh dear!" says Mama.

"Oh no!" say five little monkeys.
"Who messed up our nice, clean house?"

"I can't imagine," says Mama.
"But whoever did has plenty to do."

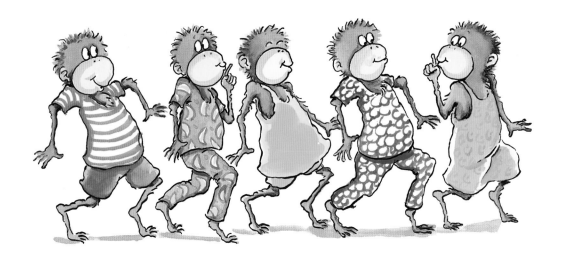

Five Little Monkeys
Bake a Birthday Cake

Five little monkeys wake up with the sun.
"Today is Mama's birthday!"

Five little monkeys tiptoe past Mama sleeping.
"Let's bake a birthday cake!"

"Sh-h-h! Don't wake up Mama!"

One little monkey reads the recipe.
"Two cups of flour. Three teaspoons of baking powder.

Sift everything together. But don't sneeze!
You'll wake up Mama!"

"Sh-h-h! Don't wake up Mama!"

Five little monkeys check on Mama.
"She's still asleep. We can finish making the cake."

One little monkey reads the recipe.

"Add four eggs."

Four little monkeys each get some eggs.

"And we need sugar and oil."
"Don't spill the oil!"

But one little monkey spills . . .

. . . and another little monkey slips and falls.
"Sh-h-h! Don't wake up Mama!"

Five little monkey check on Mama.
"She's still asleep.
We can finish making the cake."

One little monkey reads the recipe.
"Next, mix everything together and put it into pans.
Then bake the cake in the oven."

Another little monkey says, "Now we can go up to our room and make a present for Mama."

Five little monkeys start to make a present.
"Sh-h-h! Don't wake up Mama!"
One little monkey says, "Do you smell
something burning?"

Five little monkeys race past Mama sleeping.
"Sh-h-h! Don't wake up Mama!"

"Oh no! The cake dripped all over!"
"Turn off the oven!"

"Save the cake!"

"Sh-h-h! Don't wake up Mama!"

"Look here comes the fire engine!"
says one little monkey.
"Sh-h-h! Dont wake up Mama!"
says another little monkey.

"Where's the fire?" shouts a fireman.
"It's not a fire!" sniffs one little monkey.
"We ruined Mama's birthday cake."

"Wait!" says another little monkey.
"This cake doesn't taste TOO bad."
"Frosting might help," says the other fireman.

Five little monkeys and two firemen frost the cake.

"Now we can wake up Mama!"

Five little monkeys and two firemen
sing to Mama very, very, VERY, VERY LOUDLY.

And Mama wakes up!
"What a wonderful surprise," she says.
"But my birthday is tomorrow!"

"Oh no!" say five little monkeys. "But can
we still have birthday cake for breakfast?"
"Why not?" says Mama.

Five little monkeys, two firemen, and Mama think the birthday cake is delicious.

One little monkey whispers, "We can bake another cake tomorrow."

Another little monkey says, "Sh-h-h! Don't tell Mama!"

Five Little Monkeys
Wash the Car

The five little monkeys,
and Mama, can never drive far
in their rickety, rattletrap
wreck of a car.

"I've had it!" says Mama.
"Let's sell this old heap!"
She makes a big sign that says,
CAR FOR SALE—CHEAP!

Then Mama goes in.

"There's some work I should do."

"Okay," say the monkeys.

"We have work too!"

"This car is so *icky*!"

"So sticky and slimy!"

"How can we sell
an old car that's so grimy!"

"I KNOW!"
says one little monkey.

So two little monkeys
spray with a hose,
while three little monkeys
scrub the car till it glows.

"But the car is still rusty!"
"It stinks! Oh, *pee-yew*!"
"No one will buy it."
"What can we do?"

"I KNOW!"
says one little monkey.

Then four little monkeys
find paint in the shed.
Blue, yellow, and green,
purple, pink, and bright red.

They paint the old car
with designs all around,
while one little monkey
sprays perfume he found.

The five little monkeys
sit down and wait.
But no one comes by—
and it's getting late!

I KNOW!

"The car looks terrific!"
"It smells so good too!"
"Maybe no one can see it here."
"What should we do?"

"I KNOW!" says one little monkey.

So three little monkeys
start pushing the car.
The monkey who's steering
can't see very far.

Then one little monkey
shouts, "Park it right here!
Wait! It's rolling too fast!
Can't you stop? Can't you steer?"

The monkey who's steering
can't reach the brake.
The car rolls downhill to the . . .

. . . BROWN SWAMPY LAKE!

"Well, now we're in trouble!"
"We're stuck in this goo!
"We'll never get out."
"Oh, what can we do?"

"The **CROCODILES!**"
five little monkeys all shout.
One crocodile says,
"We'll help you get out!"

More crocodiles rise
from the wet swampy goo.
"We'll push this old car.
But YOU must push too."

The monkeys all quake.
"What they say isn't true!"
"They'll eat us for supper!"
"Oh, what can we do?"

"I KNOW!"
says one little monkey.

"Oh, crocodiles!" she calls.
"I heard you were strong!
But if you need *our* help,
I must have heard wrong."

"We're strong!" roar the crocs.
"We're the strongest by far!
And we can push anything
—even a car!"

So they puff and they pant
till they look very ill.
But they push that old car
to the top of the hill.

Then one monkey whispers,
"We're *still* in a stew!
If they don't go home now,
what can we do?"

"I KNOW!" says one little monkey.

"Poor crocs!" say the monkeys.
"How tired you are!
You'll never walk home!
What you need is a . . .

. . . CAR!"

The crocodiles buy it.
They pay with a check,
then climb right inside.
"We can use this old wreck!"

The monkeys all run
to tell Mama their tale.
"You might have been eaten!"
(She's turning quite pale.)

"We know!" say the monkeys.
"We're lucky, it's true.
But we *did* sell the car . . .
Can we buy one that's new?"

The five little monkeys
and Mama go shop
for a fancy new car—
with a convertible top!

And the crocodiles?
They really like their old heap.
It's such a fine car
for a long summer's . . .

...SLEEP!

Five Little Monkeys
Play Hide-and-Seek

The five little monkeys
are ready for bed
Their mama's going dancing.
She's dressed in bright red.

"Lulu's the sitter.
You'd better be good.
No tricks! No silliness!
Is that understood?"

"We'll be good!" shout the monkeys.
"We'll play hide-and-seek!
Hey Lulu, you're it!
And you'd better not peek!"

"Just one game," says Lulu.
"Then it's right off to bed.
Your bedtime's at eight.
That's what your mama said."

Lulu starts counting.

She counts up to ten.

Ready or not, here I come!

"Where are those monkeys?
Where did they go?
Where are they hiding?
I really don't know!"

But wait! . . .
"I see some fingers.
I see some toes.
I see some eyes.
I see a nose."

"No fair!" shout the monkeys.
"You found us too fast!
Let's play one more game.
And this will be the last!"

"Hold on!" says Lulu.
"It's time for bed.
'No tricks! No silliness!'
That's what your mama said."

"Oh, please," say the monkeys.
"Just one game more?
And this time can you count to
at least twenty-four?"

"Okay," sighs Lulu.
She's counted to four
when those monkeys start sneaking
right out the front door.

15 16 17 18 19 20 21 22 23 24

"Where are those monkeys?
Where did they go?
Where are they hiding?
I really don't know!"

But wait . . .
"I see some fingers.
I see some toes.
I see some eyes.
I see a nose!"

"No fair!" shout the monkeys.
"You found us too fast!
Let's play one more game.
And this will be the last!"

"Hold on!" says Lulu.
"It's time for bed.
'No tricks! No silliness!'
That's what your mama said."

But the monkeys convince her
to play one game more,
and Lulu starts counting
to one hundred and four.

"Quick!" shout the monkeys.
"We all need to hide
in a place she won't think of
—somewhere inside."

"Let's hide in the closet!"
"No, behind the chair!"
"No, under this table!"
"But she'll find us there!"

"Wait!" says one monkey.
She heads for the hall.
"I know a place
she won't think of at all!"

Lulu stops counting.
She looks all around.

"Where are those monkeys?"
There isn't a sound.

She looks behind bushes.
She searches the tree.

She hunts in the closets.
Where can they be?
Under the table?
Behind the big chair?

Those five little monkeys aren't anywhere!

"Come on, you monkeys! It's past time for bed.
'No tricks! No silliness!' That's what your mama said."

Lulu is worried. "Where *can* they be? They'll never
get to bed, and their mama will blame me!"

Just then, in comes Mama. "Did the children behave?"
"They're gone!" Lulu wails. She tries to be brave.

"Gone?" says Mama. She scratches her head. "I just
peeked in the their window, and saw them in . . .

. . . BED!"

"We fooled you!" shout the monkeys.
"Now, let's play again.
Lulu, *you* hide, and *we'll* count to ten."

"No way!" says Lulu.
"You've got to go to sleep.
But if you want to count,
I'll help you count . . .

. . . SHEEP!"

And so they start counting.
They're up to thirty-four,
when those five little monkeys
all start to snore.

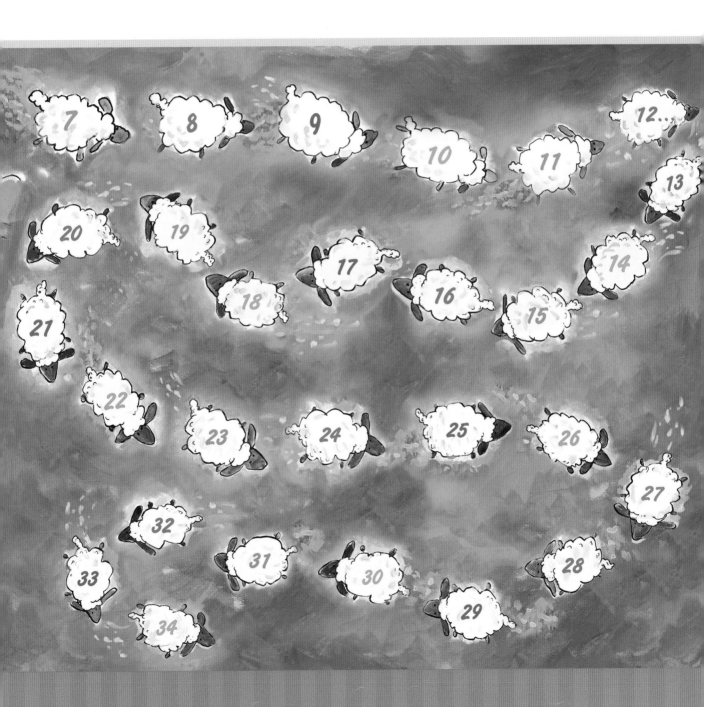

Five Little Monkeys
Jump in the Bath

Five little monkeys eat ice cream.

Lick, slurp, slop, drip, drop.

Then five little monkeys see a mud puddle!

Slippy, sloppy, goopy, gloppy!

Five icky, sticky, yucky, mucky monkeys!

"Oh no!" gasps Mama.

"Bath time for monkeys!"

Five icky, sticky, yucky, mucky monkeys take off their icky, sticky, yucky, mucky clothes.

Five icky, sticky, yucky, mucky monkeys
jump into the tub.

Splish, splatter, splash, wash, and scrub!

Five little monkeys are scrubbed and clean.

Sopping, dripping, sliding . . .

. . . slipping!

The monkeys who slipped have a good cry.

Sobbing, crying, hugging, drying.

Five little monkeys sip soup for supper.
Sip, slurp, slop . . . drip, drop.

"Thank you, Mama! Soup's delicious!"
Lots of hugs and sticky kisses . . .

Icky, sticky, yucky, mucky!

Bath time for monkeys!

Five Little Monkeys
Reading in Bed

When the five little monkeys are ready for bed,
their mama reads stories, then kisses each head.

"It's bedtime for monkeys! Now turn out the light."
"Oh, Mama! Oh, PLEASE! One more story tonight!"

But Mama's too tired. She's read more than four.
"Lights out! Sweet dreams!" She closes their door.

One monkey whispers, "This book looks so good!
If Mama won't read it, then maybe we could."

The monkeys start reading. The story is SAD.
One monkey is weeping, she's feeling so bad!

Then out come the tissues. They ALL start to bawl.
They sob and they cry till the last page of all.

It's such a good ending, their sobs turn to cheers.
Those monkeys are LOUD! (You should cover your ears!)

In fact, they're so noisy that Mama runs in.
"What's all this racket? This chaos? This din?"

One monkey admits with a guilt-ridden look,
"We've been reading the very best, happy, sad book!"

Mama raises an eyebrow. "What was it I said?"

Then one monkey sighs as she turns out the light.

"I wish we could read this new ghost book tonight."

"Just look at that goblin and mean-looking ghost!"
"It's those shadowy bats that I like the most."

One monkey starts hooting—an eerie ghost sound.
And soon they're all wailing and jumping around!

Then a dark, spooky shadow appears on the wall.
But a knock on their door is what frightens them ALL!

"It's the GHOST!" they all scream. But then . . .

. . . Mama walks in!
"What's all this racket?
This chaos? This din?"

The monkeys all gasp. "We thought YOU were the GHOST!
This book is so scary. We like it the most!"
Mama raises an eyebrow. "What was it I said?"

One monkey shivers. "That book was so creepy,

so GOOD but so scary, I'll never be sleepy!"

She pulls out a joke book. "We've got to be quiet."
But the jokes are so funny! In fact, they're a riot!

The monkeys try hard not to giggle or laugh.
But then there's a joke with a foolish giraffe.

It's so silly, so goofy, they all start to roar!

And then can you guess who flings open their door?

Oh, yes! It's Mama! She comes storming right in.
"What's all this racket? This chaos? This din?"

The monkeys keep giggling. They JUST cannot quit!
Mama picks up their books. "I've had it! That's it!"
Then she raises an eyebrow. "Did you hear what I said?"

Lights out! Sweet dreams!
No more reading in bed!

Well, the monkeys are tired. They're almost asleep when they hear someone giggle, then laugh, and then weep.

"Do you hear all that noise? And just WHO can it BE?"
"Let's sneak down the hall."
(Can you guess what they see?)

"Oh, Mama!" they giggle.

"What was it you said?"

Those monkeys are sleepy! They head out the door.

"Just wait till tomorrow, and then we'll read more!"